Madame de Toucainville's
Magnificent Hat

Northern Lights Books for Children are published by
Red Deer College Press
56 Avenue & 32 Street Box 5005
Red Deer Alberta Canada T4N 5H5

Edited for the Press by Tim Wynne-Jones.
Designed by Kunz & Associates.
Printed and bound in Korea for Red Deer College Press.
Financial support provided by the Alberta Foundation for the Arts, a beneficiary of the Lottery Fund of the Government of Alberta, and by the Canada Council, the Department of Communications and Red Deer College.

Canadian Cataloguing in Publication Data
Bland, Sue.
Madame de Toucainville's magnificent hat
(Northern lights books for children)
ISBN 0-88995-115-2
I. Title. II. Series. PS8553.L35M3 1994
jC813'.54 C93-091919-X
PZ7.B593Ma 1994

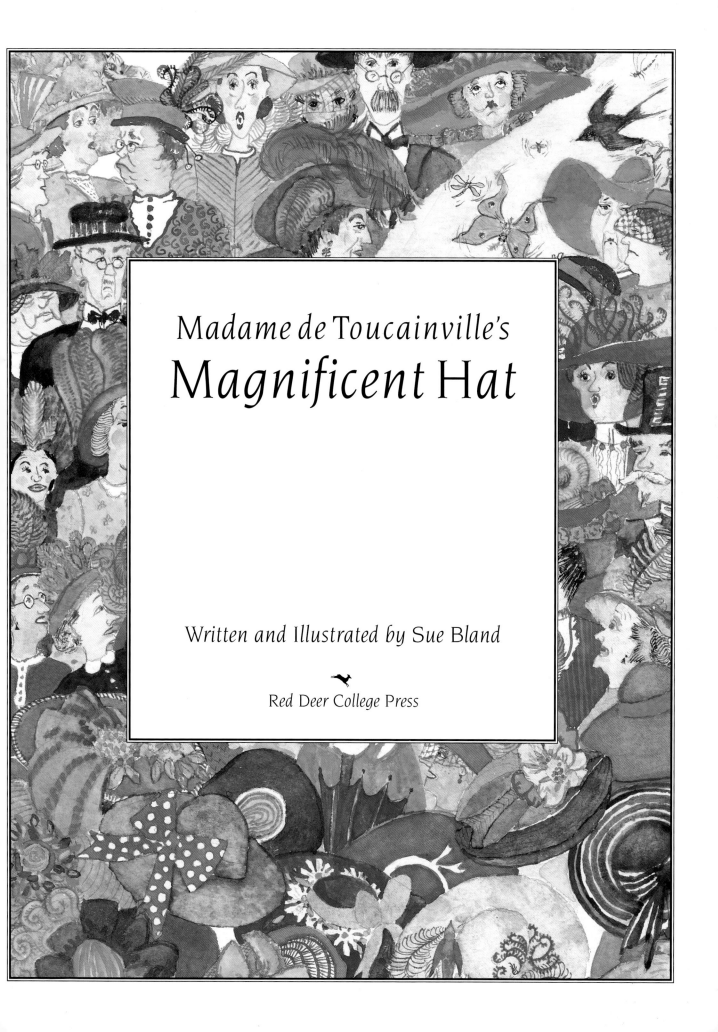

Madame de Toucainville's
Magnificent Hat

Written and Illustrated by Sue Bland

Red Deer College Press

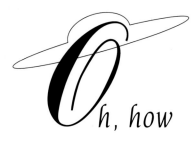

Oh, how

Madame de Toucainville loved hats.

　　She had a special hat for each of the things she loved doing best. For puttering around in the garden, a simple straw boater with goose down tucked in the ribbon.

*F*or bicycling

with Monsieur de Toucainville, a turban
with emerald ostrich plumes. And for day-
dreaming in the coulee, a yellow sailor hat
with a single peacock feather.

*M*adame's

fanciest hats were saved for the things she liked doing least. Social outings were not Madame's cup of tea, but wearing elegant headgear did give her courage.

Her sister-in-law Mathilde was a great help, especially when Madame attended meetings of the Pheasant Creek Horticultural Society. Mathilde took great care choosing exactly the right plumage. After all, Madame had a reputation to uphold. For the past four summers she had won the Bonny Bonnet Contest at the garden show. 🐞

Pheasant
Creek
Horticultural
Society
1907

*O*ne evening,

*while reading the newspaper, Monsieur de
Toucainville turned to his wife and said,
"Lucy, did you read this article about birds?"*

    She had not.

    *"It says more birds are being killed every
year just so ladies can have fancy feathers on
their hats."*

    Madame turned completely white.

"Oh, Herbert,"

she said. "In all my years of wearing hats—my
cheerful, gleeful, joyful hats—why did it never
occur to me that those gorgeous feathers had to
come from somewhere? What am I going to do?"

That night Madame dreamed that all
her hats turned into tropical birds and
flew away.

**A**fter her
dream-filled night, Madame knew exactly
what she was going to do.

"I will never buy another hat," she
announced at breakfast. "I have enough hats
to last me a lifetime."

Neither Monsieur nor Mathilde could
imagine Madame not buying new hats.

But she

kept her word. She not only stopped buying hats, she seemed to lose interest in them altogether.

Her eyes didn't sparkle quite so brightly without the ostrich plumes flying out behind her on a bike ride.

Without her straw boater, she could no longer be heard whistling happily as she pottered about in the garden.

And without her sailor hat with its single peacock feather, Madame no longer stepped so high on her way to the coulee.

Mathilde missed the fun they had choosing exactly the right hat for a public outing. These days, any old hat would do.

*T*hen came

the invitation to the Pheasant Creek Annual
Garden Show and the Bonny Bonnet Contest.

Madame de Toucainville tossed it aside,
but Mathilde and Monsieur watched as she
paced to and fro in the garden.

"I can't imagine her not entering the
contest," said Mathilde.

"Lucy never goes back on her word,"
replied Monsieur.

Madame's

spirits sagged. She never mentioned
the garden show, but it was plainly
on her mind.

Then one day, shopping in Fort
Qu'Appelle, Madame passed a
pawnbroker's shop and stopped.
Through the dusty window she could
see a hat unlike any other. The green
velvet was faded. There was a large hole
in the crown and not so much as a
ribbon or a feather to dress it up.
It was, however, the most enormous
hat Madame had ever seen.

She bought it right away.

Back at home,
Mathilde and Monsieur stared at the
hat in horror.

"I have never seen an uglier hat in all my
life," said Mathilde.

Astonished, they watched Madame pick
it up and dance around the room, laughing
out loud.

"Oh, it may be a little worn," she said,
"but just you wait and see how we can make
it come alive again!"

*M*adame led
them out to the garden.

They covered the green velvet with so many blossoms that the hat grew to an alarming size.

What a lark they had!

A butterfly came by. A ladybug. Then bumblebees and dragonflies. Why, even a hummingbird could be seen drinking nectar from a bleeding heart. ❦

*T*he day

of the garden show, Mathilde had quite a time
trying to pin the enormous hat to Madame's
head. As she watched in the mirror, Madame
thought she had never felt more magnificent.

"I declare," said Miss Whippet, "that hat
is moving."

"It looks just like her flower garden,"
snorted Mrs. Beebottom.

"Is that a real goldfinch?" asked Mrs.
Wright.

"Impossible!" sputtered Mrs. Beebottom.

They could not take their eyes off the
astonishing hat. And so it was that Madame
de Toucainville won the Bonny Bonnet
Contest for the fifth year running.

On the way

home, tired but happy, Madame decided to
take off her magnificent hat. After all, it was
heavy. But no sooner did she lift it from her
head than a strong gust of wind swept it into
the sky. She tried to catch it, but the hat was
doing a dance all its own. Madame and
Monsieur watched helplessly as the
magnificent hat twirled and whirled and
disappeared somewhere over the coulee. ❦

_M_adame

searched relentlessly for days, but she
never did find her magnificent hat.

After one particularly long and
pleasant expedition, she returned home
with a large basketful of flowers and
juicy saskatoon berries. As she emptied
its contents onto the floor, she said to
Monsieur, "Just look at the treasures I
have found . . . I'm beginning to think
that my hat isn't really lost at all.
It has become a part of the prairies.
And maybe that is where it really
belongs."